SIX DEGREES OF SPORTS

SIX DEGREES° OF DAVID ORTIZ

CONNECTING BASEBALL STARS

BY TYLER OMOTH

CAPSTONE PRESS
a capstone imprint

Sports Illustrated Six Degrees of Sports are published by Capstone Press, 1710 Roe Crest Drive, North Mankato, Minnesota 56003.
www.capstonepub.com

Library of Congress Cataloging-in-Publication Data
Cataloging information on file with the Library of Congress
ISBN 978-1-4914-2142-0 (Library Binding)

Editorial Credits
Nate LeBoutillier, editor; Ted Williams, designer; Eric Gohl, media researcher; Katy LaVigne, production specialist

Photo Credits
Corbis: Bettmann, 28 (bottom); CriaImages.com: Jay Robert Nash Collection, 10 (bottom), 12 (Robinson); Getty Images: Focus on Sport, 33, NY Daily News Archive/ Charles Hoff, 35; Library of Congress: cover (Gehrig, Ruth), 6 (Gehrig, Ruth), 11, 18 (Cobb), 23 (bottom), 24 (Young), 29; Newscom: Everett Collection, 12 (Aaron), Icon SMI/Gavin Baker, 32 (bottom), Icon SMI/John McDonough, 18 (Coleman), Icon SMI/Mark LoMoglio, 19, 20 (top), Icon SMI/Sporting News, 40 (bottom), Icon SMI/ TSN, 24 (Paige), 36 (Fingers), SportsChrome/PM, 21, ZUMA Press/Brian Peterson, 30 (Puckett), ZUMA Press/Malcolm W. Emmons, 17 (top); Sports Illustrated: Al Tielemans, 4–5, 6 (background), 12 (Thome), 20 (bottom), 30 (Hunter, background), 32 (background), 36 (Chapman, Papelbon), 39 (top), Damian Strohmeyer, cover (Ortiz, Jeter), 1, 6 (Ortiz, Jeter), 7, 8 (top), 15, 18 (Ellsbury, background), 20 (background), 22 (background), 31, 32 (top), David E. Klutho, 12 (Cabrera), 18 (McCutchen), 30 (Pedroia), Heinz Kluetmeier, 18 (Henderson), 22, 36 (Eckersley), 41, John Biever, 12 (background), 36 (background), 38, John D. Hanlon, 18 (Brock), 23 (top), John G. Zimmerman, 24 (Koufax), 28 (top), 30 (Mays), John Iacono, 10 (top), 16, 24 (Ryan), 27 (bottom), John W. McDonough, 14 (top), 37, Manny Millan, 30 (Smith), 34 (top), Richard Meek, 17 (bottom), Robert Beck, cover (Ripken, Trout), 6 (Ripken, Trout), 8 (bottom), 9, 12 (Pujols), 13, 14 (bottom), 24 (Kershaw, background), 25, 26, 36 (Hoffman), 39 (bottom), 40 (top), Simon Bruty, 24 (Verlander), 27 (top), 36 (Rivera), Walter Iooss Jr., 12 (Jackson), 30 (Bench), 34 (bottom)

Design Elements
Shutterstock

Source Notes
Page 15: "Jim Thome: What They Say." www.jockbio.com/Bios/Thome/Thome_theysay.html; Page 17: "Aaron, Hank: Baseball Hall of Fame." www.baseballhall.org/hof/aaron-hank; Page 20: "Jacoby Ellsbury ties MLB fielding record in win." *The Boston Globe*. 21 May 2009. www.bostonglobe.com/sports/2009/05/21/jacoby-ellsbury-ties-mlb-fielding-record-win/GlHBzabAehUbOTJ2GdAxnK/story.html; Page 40: "Dennis Eckersley: The National Pastime Museum." www.thenationalpastimemuseum.com/article/my-favorite-player-dennis-eckersley

Printed in the United States of America in Stevens Point, Wisconsin.
112014 008479WZS15

TABLE OF CONTENTS

REMINDS ME OF . . .

David Ortiz saunters up to the batter's box. He digs out a spot with his cleats, claps his hands, waggles his bat like the tail of a cat. The pitcher delivers. Ortiz swings, and bat meets ball like a clap of thunder. The ball arcs high into the air and lands in some lucky fan's glove—yet another game-winning home run. He has done more than just bash a homer, though. He has brought you to your feet—or to your knees. He has coaxed a roar from your throat—unless he's left you speechless. He's moved you. And whether you say it out loud or not, what you're thinking is, *I've never seen that before.*

But someone has seen it before. This is just about the time your father says, ***"Reminds me of Reggie Jackson."***

To which your grandfather, eyes twinkling, might have said, ***"Reminds me of Mickey Mantle."***

To which your great-grandfather, grin spreading, might have said, ***"Reminds me of Babe Ruth."***

Maybe it was an uncle or an aunt who made the comparison. It could have been anyone, right? One element of sports that trickles down through generations is that we love to connect the players of the game. We measure greatness in sports by the records we keep. But we also measure greatness by way of comparison and contrast. We bring together what may be separate by remembering, *Hey, those guys played together for a couple seasons on the same team*, or, *Hey, that guy actually broke the other guy's record!* These types of connections are what this book is all about.

So whether you talk baseball in barbershops or coffee shops, this book is for you. Whether you strike up debate in back rooms, parlor rooms, living rooms, chat rooms, or lunchrooms, on the streets or in the bleachers, with your friends or foes or teachers, Six Degrees of Sports is for you. Please enjoy it, and make your own connections.

CHAPTER ONE

SIX DEGREES OF DAVID ORTIZ

HALL OF FAME HEROES

Major League Baseball has always had talented ballplayers who excel at things like clubbing home runs or swiping bases. Then there are those who seem to be a cut above. These players are some of the game's very best. They go beyond hitting, running, catching, and throwing. They seem to shine brightest when their teams need them most. And they do it year in and year out in heroic fashion. If they aren't in the Hall of Fame already, they soon will be.

HEIGHT: 6-4 **WEIGHT:** 230 lbs.
BATS: Left **THROWS:** Left
BORN: 11/18/1975 in Santo Domingo, Dominican Republic
SCOUTING REPORT: Big Papi swings a big bat. Heavy hitter famous for launching towering home runs when it seems to matter the most.

▸ **David Ortiz** is all smiles when he's playing baseball. Not known for his defense or his speed, Ortiz does one thing, and he does it very well. He hits the ball. Since arriving in Boston in 2003, he has been a crowd favorite and a constant threat in the middle of the club's lineup, peaking with 54 home runs in 2006. Big games bring out the best in "Big Papi," known for clutch home runs. In three World Series appearances he has a .455 batting average and a .576 slugging percentage, both considerably better than his regular season stats. In 2013 he led the Red Sox to a World Series trophy and was named the World Series Most Valuable Player (MVP).

▸ **Mike Trout** wasted no time endearing himself to Los Angeles Angels fans. He's a big, muscular player with an All-American smile, but there's more than just power to his game. This Trout can fly. During his

HEIGHT: 6-2 **WEIGHT:** 230 lbs.
BATS: Right **THROWS:** Right
BORN: 08/07/1991 in Vineland, N.J.
SCOUTING REPORT: Talented Angel displays heavenly repertoire of skills in all aspects of the game as one of baseball's brightest young stars.

rookie campaign he swiped a league-best 49 stolen bases and wowed the crowd with show-stopping catches in center field. He won the American League (AL) Rookie of the Year Award and nearly beat out veteran slugger Miguel Cabrera for AL MVP. Spectacular catches, booming home runs, and swiped bases—it's rare to see a player so young do so many things so well. In 2014 the 23-year-old phenom won AL MVP, becoming the youngest player to ever win the MVP by a unanimous vote.

The New York Yankees won five World Series titles between 1996 and 2009. It's no coincidence that ▶ **Derek Jeter** took over the shortstop position in 1995. A 13-time All-Star, Jeter was the model of consistency. However, what Jeter is best known for is his leadership on and off the field.

YANKEES

DEREK JETER
▶ Shortstop

HEIGHT: 6-3 **WEIGHT:** 195 lbs.
BATS: Right **THROWS:** Right
BORN: 06/26/1974 in Pequannock, N.J.
SCOUTING REPORT: Pinstriped shortstop was the model of consistent greatness and leadership over a 20-year Yankee career.

Though he wasn't a premier power hitter, Jeter's clutch bat was deadly when the game was on the line. The Yankees named him team captain in 2003. Jeter held that honor for more than a decade as he showed his teammates how to win with hustle, heart, and smart play.

Fans of the Baltimore Orioles during the 1980s and '90s had a pretty sweet deal going. They knew they could always find at least three sure things at the ballpark: green grass, hot dogs, and ▸ **Cal Ripken Jr.** Bigger than most shortstops of the time, Ripken was a remarkable athlete who played his position with as much intelligence as pure athletic ability. On September 6th, 1995, he broke a record that had been in the record books for 56 years by playing in his 2,131st game consecutively, earning his nickname "The Iron Man." The 19-time All-Star was inducted into the Baseball Hall of Fame in 2007.

ORIOLES

CAL RIPKEN JR.
▶ Shortstop

HEIGHT: 6-4 **WEIGHT:** 200 lbs.
BATS: Right **THROWS:** Right
BORN: 08/24/1960 in Havre de Grace, Md.
SCOUTING REPORT: "Iron Man" Cal was as tough and dependable as he was talented in 21 seasons with the O's.

The Golden Era of the New York Yankees during the late 1920s and 1930s was filled with brash personalities, spectacular hitters, and six World Series titles. None were as consistent as the relentless ▸ **Lou Gehrig**. His height and build were both average. But when Gehrig played baseball, his talent and dogged work ethic took over. He was the quiet leader in a clubhouse full of superstars, and he held the team together. He amassed 493 home runs in a career sadly shortened by a disease of the nervous system,

YANKEES

LOU GEHRIG
▶ First Base

HEIGHT: 6-0 **WEIGHT:** 200 lbs.
BATS: Left **THROWS:** Left
BORN: 06/19/1903 in New York, N.Y.
SCOUTING REPORT: The Iron Horse was a reliable hitting machine and team leader during the Yankees golden era of the 1920s and 1930s.

later named Lou Gehrig's Disease. During his retirement speech, he inspired many as he proclaimed, "… today I consider myself the luckiest man on the face of the earth."

Flashy and confident to a fault, ▸ **Babe Ruth** was every bit as spectacular as Gehrig was reliable. Ruth began his career as a pitcher with the Boston Red Sox and was no slouch. He won 23 games in 1921, 24 in 1922, and 94 over the course of a 10-year pitching career. However, it was his bat that made Babe Ruth a baseball legend. He was a powerful hitter who pounded 714 career home runs and 2,214 runs batted in (RBIs). The Babe looked more like a couch potato than a professional athlete. But when he stepped onto the baseball field, he was a slugging, hard throwing, and remarkable athlete. Arguably the best all-around player to ever play the game, George Herman "Babe" Ruth is a name synonymous with greatness.

YANKEES

GEORGE HERMAN "BABE" RUTH

▸ Outfield and Pitcher

HEIGHT: 6-2 **WEIGHT:** 215 lbs.
BATS: Left **THROWS:** Left
BORN: 02/06/1895 in Baltimore, Md.
SCOUTING REPORT: The Bambino could pitch and play outfield, but hitting home runs was what he did best—with mythological might and style.

FACT

Babe Ruth started his career with the Boston Red Sox—the same team for which David Ortiz stars.

CHAPTER TWO

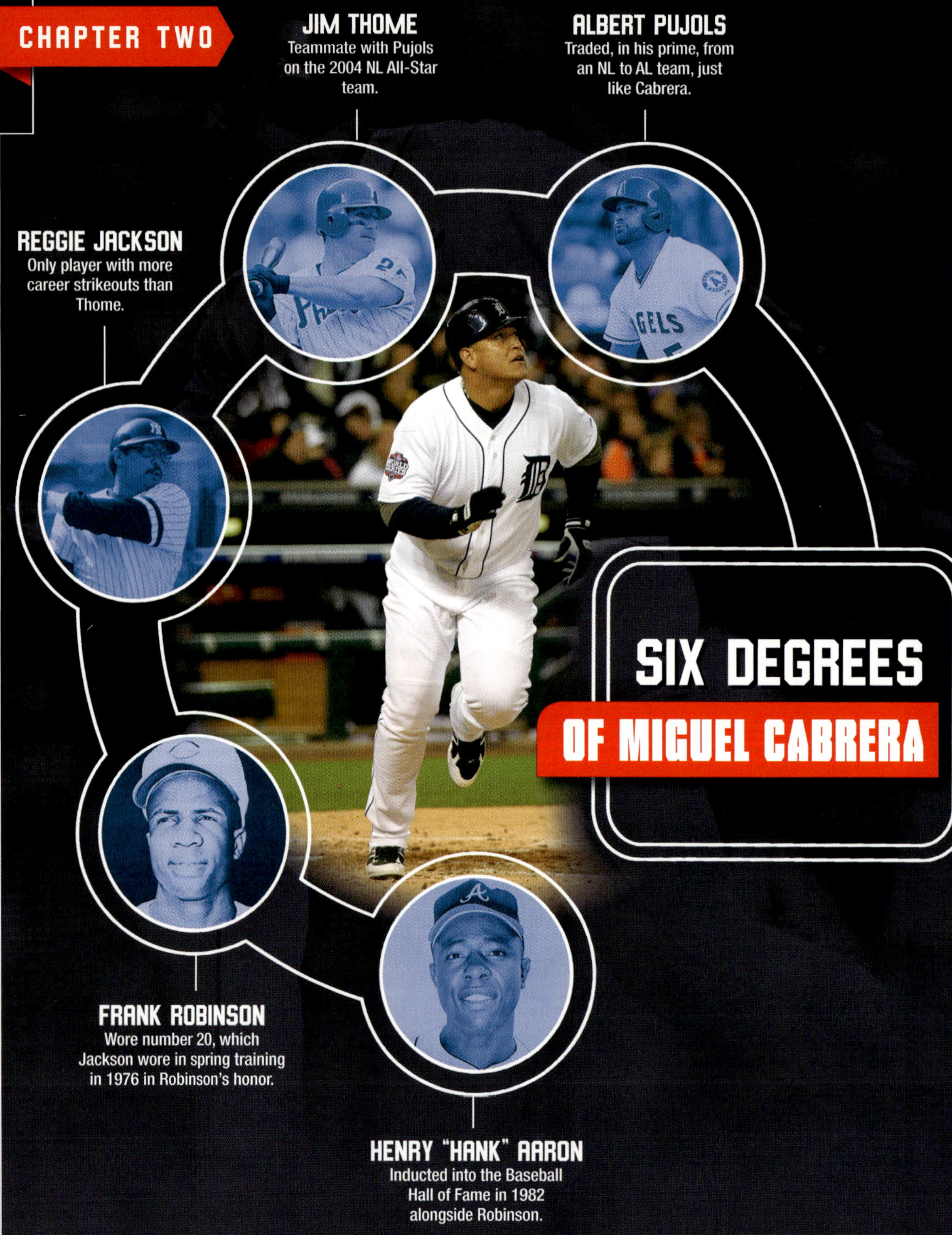
JIM THOME
Teammate with Pujols on the 2004 NL All-Star team.
ALBERT PUJOLS
Traded, in his prime, from an NL to AL team, just like Cabrera.
REGGIE JACKSON
Only player with more career strikeouts than Thome.
SIX DEGREES
OF MIGUEL CABRERA
FRANK ROBINSON
Wore number 20, which Jackson wore in spring training in 1976 in Robinson's honor.
HENRY "HANK" AARON
Inducted into the Baseball Hall of Fame in 1982 alongside Robinson.

SUPER SLUGGERS

Baseball fans love the long ball. It's thrilling to watch a player change the game with one mighty swing of his bat. These sluggers make pitchers cringe and outfielders play with their backs up against the wall. They won't bunt, and they're not looking for a walk. They come out swinging.

▶ **Miguel Cabrera** burst onto the baseball scene in 2003 at just 20 years old with a baby face and a big smile. Fans loved him from the start. In his very first Major League game he hit a walk-off home run to straightaway center field to win in extra innings. The home runs just kept coming after that. In 2012 he became the first player to win the Triple Crown since 1967 by leading the league in home runs, RBIs, and batting average. Cabrera, a fun-loving teammate from the very beginning of his career, has always enjoyed a joke with his coaches or the media.

▶ **Albert Pujols** hit the Major League Baseball scene by blasting 37 homers and tallying 130 RBIs on his way to National League (NL) Rookie of the Year honors in 2001. With a wide stance and mammoth arms, Pujols is an intimidating presence at the plate.

TIGERS

MIGUEL CABRERA

▶ Third Base

HEIGHT: 6-4 **WEIGHT:** 240 lbs.
BATS: Right **THROWS:** Right
BORN: 04/18/1983 in Maracay, Venezuela
SCOUTING REPORT: Hits for average and huge power. Every year he's a threat to win the MVP.

ANGELS

ALBERT PUJOLS

▶ First Base

HEIGHT: 6-3 **WEIGHT:** 230 lbs.
BATS: Right **THROWS:** Right
BORN: 01/16/1980 in Santo Domingo, Dominican Republic
SCOUTING REPORT: One of the best pure hitters of his generation, he can do it all with amazing strength.

Though he looked like he could be the linebacker on a football team, his knowledge of hitting and pure strength has made him one of the most dominating hitters in history. On September 10th, 2011, Pujols tied a Major League record by blasting three home runs in Game 3 of the World Series against the Texas Rangers.

In 2011 the elite 600 home run club welcomed a new member—a hulking lumberjack of a lefty named ▸ **Jim Thome**. Thome spent much of his career as a designated hitter. A gentle giant, he was one of baseball's friendliest guys. He was polite to teammates, opponents, and even reporters. But when he was standing in the batter's box, he simply crushed fastballs. He retired as seventh on the all-time home run list with 612 longballs to his name. Former Cleveland Indians owner John Hart summed him up saying, "He's got that 'aw gee, aw shucks' air about him. Jim is Huck Finn personified, and he really likes to play baseball."

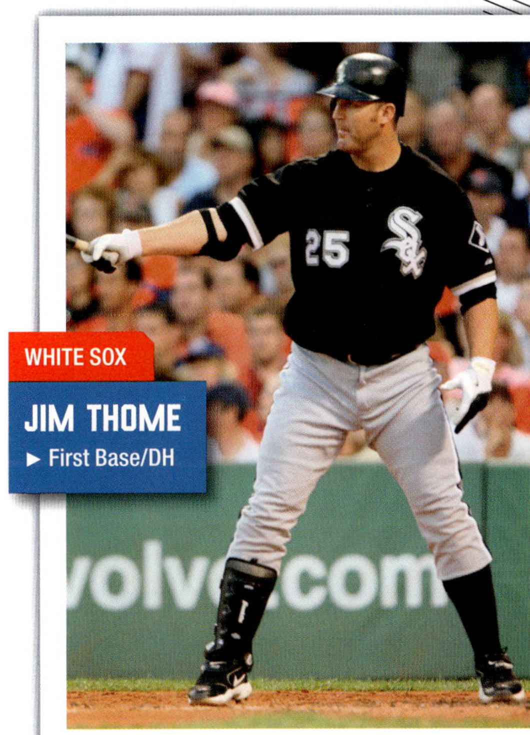

WHITE SOX

JIM THOME
▸ First Base/DH

HEIGHT: 6-4 **WEIGHT:** 250 lbs.
BATS: Left **THROWS:** Right
BORN: 08/27/1970 in Peoria, Ill.
SCOUTING REPORT: Gentle Giant's huge home run stroke won him many a fan.

FACT

Jim Thome played for six different teams. He hit 65 homers against the Detroit Tigers alone.

HEIGHT: 6-0 **WEIGHT:** 195 lbs.
BATS: Left **THROWS:** Left
BORN: 05/18/1946 in Wyncote, Pa.
SCOUTING REPORT: Mr. October is a pure power hitter with a personality as big as his bat.

Another powerful lefty who liked to swing and swing hard was ▸ **Reggie Jackson**. When he missed, his powerful follow-through would almost corkscrew him right out of the batter's box. Crushing 563 home runs over his career, Jackson wasn't just an everyday masher—he was Mr. October. Jackson wasn't afraid to talk big, and he backed it up. As a Yankee he became the first player to hit three home runs in one World Series game in Game 6 of the 1977 World Series. Jackson respected the great hitters that came before him. In 1976, he wore the number 20 in honor of retiring legend Frank Robinson.

▸ **Frank Robinson** was more than just a bruising hitter, he was one of the best all-around players of his time. As smart as he was talented, Robinson was always at full-speed on the field, trying to make the impossible catch or take an extra base. In 1961 he led the Cincinnati Reds to the pennant, winning the NL MVP. He ran away with the AL MVP in 1966 after winning the batting Triple Crown with the Baltimore Orioles. Robinson is still

ORIOLES

FRANK ROBINSON

► Outfield

HEIGHT: 6-1 **WEIGHT:** 190 lbs.
BATS: Right **THROWS:** Right
BORN: 08/31/1935 in Beaumont, Tex.
SCOUTING REPORT: All-around gamer hits for power and average and makes his teams better by leading.

the only player to win MVP in both leagues. His 586 career home runs put him ninth on the all-time list.

▸ **Henry Aaron** is arguably the greatest home run hitter of all time. Hammerin' Hank, as he is more commonly known, pounded 755 career home runs, a record that stood for 33 years. He is still the record holder for career RBIs (2,297), total bases (6,856), and extra base hits (1,477). He was remarkably consistent over his career, earning All-Star honors 21 times. Twenty-year National League pitcher Curt Simmons said, "Trying to throw a fastball by Henry Aaron is like trying to sneak a sunrise past a rooster." Many pitchers tried, but few were successful.

BRAVES

HENRY "HANK" AARON

► Outfield and First Base

HEIGHT: 6-0 **WEIGHT:** 180 lbs.
BATS: Right **THROWS:** Right
BORN: 02/05/1934 in Mobile, Ala.
SCOUTING REPORT: Remarkably consistent run-producer and home run hitter also plays Gold Glove defense.

CHAPTER THREE

SIX DEGREES OF JACOBY ELLSBURY

STEALTHY SPEEDSTERS

Only 90 feet separate first base from second base. For this group of elite speedsters, that's just too close to resist. This class of super sprinters use their speed to help themselves to another base, and sometimes more. They give pitchers fits and dance in the nightmares of catchers. These are the elite base stealers.

YANKEES

JACOBY ELLSBURY
▶ Outfield

HEIGHT: 6-1 **WEIGHT:** 195 lbs.
BATS: Left **THROWS:** Left
BORN: 09/11/1983 in Madras, Ore.
SCOUTING REPORT: Pure burner uses his speed to rack up big offensive numbers and play a stellar outfield.

▶ **Jacoby Ellsbury's** career really hit the ground running. During his rookie year in Boston in 2008 he led the AL with 50 stolen bases. His sophomore season he did even better by swiping the top spot in stolen bases (70) and triples (10). Ellsbury doesn't leave all his speed on the base paths, though. He also uses it to chase down gap shots and make unbelievable plays in centerfield. Ex-Red Sox teammate Jason Bay said, "He's one of those guys who is athletic and fast, and he knows how to play the outfield. He's fun to watch, especially in right-center. There's a lot of room [at Fenway Park] ... to see him get after it."

If you were to go to a baseball game at Pittsburgh's PNC Park, you'd see ▶ **Andrew McCutchen** gliding across center field with his long, dark dreadlocks trailing behind in the wind.

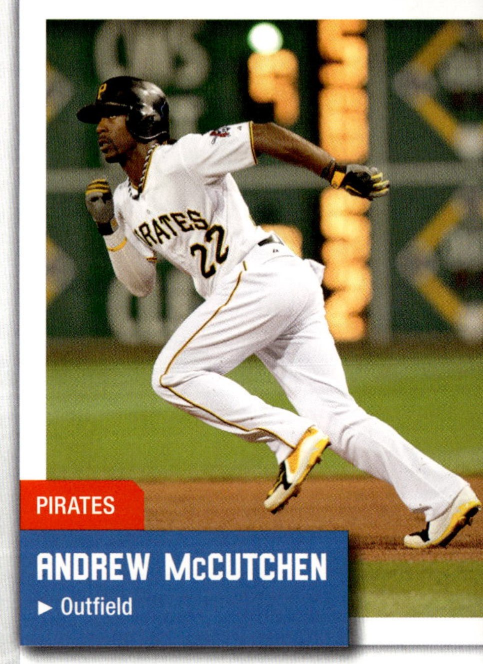

PIRATES

ANDREW McCUTCHEN
▶ Outfield

HEIGHT: 5-10 **WEIGHT:** 190 lbs.
BATS: Right **THROWS:** Right
BORN: 10/10/1986 in Fort Meade, Fla.
SCOUTING REPORT: Five-tool Buc brings speed, power, defense, batting average, and a great arm to the park every day.

In 2013 he hit for a .317 batting average while clubbing 21 home runs and stealing 27 bases, earning him the NL MVP award. He wears his pants long, but if you look closely you may get a glimpse of his crazy socks. In one game in 2013 he wore zebra-striped socks. Maybe unleashing his inner animal is how he became a three-time NL All-Star.

▸ **Vince Coleman** was a threat to steal bases from the moment he put on his major league spikes. At just 170 pounds, the lean sprinter ran away with the 1985 NL Rookie of the Year Award by swiping a whopping 110 bases, the most ever by a rookie. Coleman wreaked havoc as a leadoff hitter. Using his speed to get on base, he would torment pitchers with daring leads off of first. He continued to run his way into the record books. He was so adept at swiping bags that he once stole 50 consecutive bases without being thrown out, another MLB record.

CARDINALS

VINCE COLEMAN

▸ Outfield

HEIGHT: 6-0 **WEIGHT:** 170 lbs.
BATS: Both **THROWS:** Right
BORN: 09/22/1961 in Jacksonville, Fla.
SCOUTING REPORT: Pure base-stealer possesses a great first step with speed to spare.

FACT

Vince Coleman stole more than 100 bases in each of his first three seasons.

HEIGHT: 5-10 **WEIGHT:** 190 lbs.
BATS: Right **THROWS:** Left
BORN: 12/25/1958 in Chicago, Ill.
SCOUTING REPORT: Pure athlete remodeled the leadoff hitter position and became the best base stealer in history.

▸ **Rickey Henderson** dared pitchers to find his strike zone by crouching very low. While he was lean enough to be amazingly fast, he also packed a lot of muscle. If they threw a strike, he could hit it into the outfield seats with power that few leadoff hitters before him possessed. If the pitcher walked him, he would terrorize him on the base paths, stealing bases with his trademark head-first slide. The "Man of Steal" broke Lou Brock's all-time stolen base record in 1991 by stealing his 939th base. Henderson retired with 1,406 stolen bases, a lofty record that some say may never be broken.

▸ **Lou Brock** could hit and hit for power. But when he was on the bases, he caused a lot of trouble for opposing pitchers. In 1964 his manager, Johnny Keane, asked him to stop swinging for the fences and focus on wreaking havoc with his speed. Brock obliged by studying the art of stealing bases and became the greatest base thief of his generation. He stole more than 50 bases for 12 consecutive years in a row (1965–1976) and helped the St. Louis Cardinals win two World Series titles.

HEIGHT: 6-0 **WEIGHT:** 170 lbs.
BATS: Left **THROWS:** Left
BORN: 06/18/1939 in El Dorado, Ark.
SCOUTING REPORT: Fine for-average hitter revolutionized the art of base stealing.

Brock broke Ty Cobb's career stolen base record and retired as the all-time leader with 938 stolen bases.

▸ **Ty Cobb** was a merciless competitor. He looked for weakness in his opponents and then capitalized on it. Cobb was average in height and build, but surpassed all of his peers in intensity. He amassed an amazing 4,191 hits during his career, a record that stood for 57 years. Cobb was smart, fearless, and remarkably aggressive on the base paths. Shortstops and second basemen knew that when he was stealing second, he'd come in with his cleats up, daring them to get in his way. There were some rumors that he even sharpened his cleats. He was so fearless that he even stole home a record 54 times. In an era when home runs were not as common, Ty Cobb used his legs to become baseball's first truly great base stealer.

HEIGHT: 6-1 **WEIGHT:** 175 lbs.
BATS: Left **THROWS:** Right
BORN: 12/18/1886 in Narrows, Ga.
SCOUTING REPORT: Fierce competitor was known for his talent, intelligence, competitiveness, and ruthless effort in the game.

CHAPTER FOUR

SIX DEGREES OF CLAYTON KERSHAW

NOLAN RYAN
Boyhood idol of Verlander.

JUSTIN VERLANDER
Won first AL Cy Young Award in 2011, same year that Kershaw won first NL Cy Young.

SANDY KOUFAX
Only player besides Ryan to have more strikeouts than innings in his career.

LEROY "SATCHEL" PAIGE
Like Koufax, named to the MLB All-Century team in 2000.

DENTON TRUE "CY" YOUNG
Namesake of the Cy Young Award given for best pitcher, which some have lobbied to change to Satchel Paige Award.

ASTOUNDING ACES

Good pitchers control games, but great pitchers dominate them. They use blazing fastballs and incredible breaking pitches to make even the best hitters look foolish. They stop losing streaks, set records, and keep fans on the edge of their seats. These are baseball's best pitchers. These are baseball's aces.

HEIGHT: 6-3 **WEIGHT:** 195 lbs.
BATS: Left **THROWS:** Left
BORN: 03/19/1988 in Dallas, Tex.
SCOUTING REPORT: Southpaw with a giant curveball and a live fastball never lets batters get comfortable in the box.

▶ **Clayton Kershaw** is a control freak. He doesn't have the rocket arm of some fastball pitchers, but his devastating 12-to-6 curveball, which dives straight down, more than makes up for it. Kershaw has pinpoint control of all of his pitches, allowing him to throw them for called strikes or to lure hitters into swinging hopelessly. He earned the NL Cy Young Award in 2011 and won it again in 2013 with a microscopic 1.83 ERA in 236 innings pitched. In 2014 Kershaw threw his first career no-hitter, won the Cy Young for the third time, and was voted NL MVP, a rare feat for a pitcher.

▶ **Justin Verlander** is an imposing presence on the mound. At 6 foot 5 inches and 225 pounds, he looks every bit the part of a power pitcher. Verlander is a strikeout artist whose fastball has been clocked as high as 101 miles per hour. If that weren't enough, he

FACT

Clayton Kershaw won the Cy Young in 2013 and 2014, but lost four playoff games to the Cardinals.

TIGERS

JUSTIN VERLANDER

▶ Starting Pitcher

HEIGHT: 6-5 **WEIGHT:** 225 lbs.
BATS: Right **THROWS:** Right
BORN: 02/20/1983 in Manakin-Sabot, Va.
SCOUTING REPORT: Fireballing right-hander also tosses a big curve that dominates hitters and games.

has a knee-buckling curveball and a good change-up to keep hitters guessing. In 2011 he dominated the league with 24 wins, 250 strikeouts, and a stellar 2.40 earned run average (ERA). This pitcher's triple crown earned him both the AL Cy Young award and the AL MVP.

Hitters who faced "The Ryan Express" usually got a one-way ticket right back to the bench. When ▶ **Nolan Ryan** pitched, his windup was exaggerated. His arms went behind his head, and his leg kick was so high his knee almost touched his face. Nolan Ryan is the all-time MLB strikeout king with 5,417 whiffs in his career. With a blazing fastball, he threw a record seven no-hitters. In 27 seasons in the bigs, Ryan pitched 5,386 total innings, making him the only pitcher other than Sandy Koufax to have more strikeouts than innings in his career.

RANGERS

NOLAN RYAN

▶ Starting Pitcher

HEIGHT: 6-2 **WEIGHT:** 185 lbs.
BATS: Right **THROWS:** Right
BORN: 01/31/1947 in Refugio, Tex.
SCOUTING REPORT: Tough-as-nails competitor has an epic fastball that makes him the king of strikeouts and no-hitters.

Considered the best lefthander that baseball has ever seen, ▸ **Sandy Koufax** was the master of the sweeping curveball. With a vicious drop, his curve would go chin to shin and leave batters shaking their heads. His 382 strikeouts in 1965 are the most ever in a season by a lefthander. Koufax won 25 or more games three times and rarely left the mound until the game was finished. In 1965 Koufax earned the World Series MVP by pitching in three games and dominating Game 7 on just two days of rest. However, at the young age of 30, his elbow began to hurt, and he walked away from the game after just 12 seasons.

DODGERS

SANDY KOUFAX

▸ Starting Pitcher

HEIGHT: 6-2 **WEIGHT:** 210 lbs.
BATS: Right **THROWS:** Left
BORN: 12/30/1935 in Brooklyn, N.Y.
SCOUTING REPORT: One of baseball's best lefties flings the nastiest curveball around.

▸ **Satchel Paige** had a mouth that ran as fast as his heater. Because of racial discrimination, he didn't play in the Major Leagues until 1948, when he was 41 years old. From 1927 to 1947, Paige dominated the

BROWNS

SATCHEL PAIGE

▸ Starting Pitcher

HEIGHT: 6-3 **WEIGHT:** 180 lbs.
BATS: Right **THROWS:** Right
BORN: July 7, 1906 in Mobile, Ala.
SCOUTING REPORT: Lanky righty whose big personality compliments a fantastic ability to strike 'em out.

Negro Leagues with a blazing fastball and pinpoint control, also attacking hitters with colorfully named pitches like his change-up, the "two-hump blooper." He was so confident that he would tell his fielders to go to the dugout and then strike out the side. Paige was elected to the Hall of Fame in 1971, the first Negro League player to enter the Hall.

When ▸ **Cy Young** tried out for a professional baseball team in 1889, he pitched to a hitter against the backstop. His barrage of fastballs splintered the wood backstop so badly that the team's manager said that it "looked like a cyclone had just passed." From that point on, everyone called Trenton "Cy." Over his remarkable career, Cy Young amassed 511 wins, topping 30 wins in five different seasons. He also believed in finishing what he started, collecting 749 complete games. Over a century later, he still holds the records for most wins and complete games. Today, the best pitcher in each league is given an award that is the mark of a true ace, the Cy Young Award.

SPIDERS

DENTON TRUE "CY" YOUNG

▸ Starting Pitcher

HEIGHT: 6-2 **WEIGHT:** 210 lbs.
BATS: Right **THROWS:** Right
BORN: 03/29/1967 in Gilmore, Ohio
SCOUTING REPORT: Durable and consistent innings-eating machine racks up wins unlike any other pitcher in history.

CHAPTER FIVE
KIRBY PUCKETT
Patrolled Metrodome center field in Minnesota before passing the torch to Hunter.
TORII HUNTER
Winner of the "Heart and Hustle" award in 2011, which Pedroia took home in 2013.
OZZIE SMITH
Played against Puckett in the 1987 World Series.
SIX DEGREES
OF DUSTIN PEDROIA
JOHNNY BENCH
Teammate with Ozzie Smith on the 1983 NL All-Star Team
WILLIE MAYS
Six-time NL All-Star teammate of Bench.

GLORIOUS GLOVE MEN

Whether it's a diving stop or a wall-climbing leap to rob a home run, great defensive plays bring the crowd to its feet and make pitchers breathe a sigh of relief. These are the players with the soft hands, great instincts, and remarkable athleticism to make the plays that ordinary players cannot. These are baseball's great glove men.

RED SOX

DUSTIN PEDROIA

▶ Second Base

HEIGHT: 5-8 **WEIGHT:** 165 lbs.
BATS: Right **THROWS:** Right
BORN: 08/17/1983 in Woodland, Calif.
SCOUTING REPORT: Sparkplug of a player swings a big bat and plays superb defense at second base.

At only 5 foot 8 inches tall, ▶ **Dustin Pedroia** plays baseball with the heart of a giant. A surprising slugger, he won the 2007 AL Rookie of the Year and the 2008 AL MVP awards. Where Pedroia's passion for baseball really comes out is when he's wearing his glove. As a second baseman, he has a lot of turf to cover. His uniform is usually dirty from diving and sliding in the dirt, making every play that he can. Great plays are fun, but he believes it's preparing for the routine plays that makes him a great fielder.

▶ **Torii Hunter's** earned the nickname "Spider-Man" by scaling outfield walls to rob home runs. A solid all-around player with a big smile, Hunter patrols the outfield with cat-like reflexes and agility. Hunter won nine consecutive AL Gold Glove awards from 2001 to 2009. In 2002 he brought his skills to the MLB All-Star

TIGERS

TORII HUNTER

▶ Outfield

HEIGHT: 6-2 **WEIGHT:** 225 lbs.
BATS: Right **THROWS:** Right
BORN: 07/18/1975 in Pine Bluff, Ark.
SCOUTING REPORT: Nimble outfielder who gets a great jump on fly balls and makes spectacular catches at and above the wall.

Game. When Barry Bonds of the National League crushed a ball out to centerfield, Hunter tracked it down and made a mighty leap high over the wall to rob the home run.

In every aspect of the game, ▸ **Kirby Puckett** was all hustle. He stood only 5 foot 8 inches tall and had a stocky body shaped like a fire hydrant. But he ran well, had a strong, accurate throwing arm, and had a great sense of timing when jumping to rob hits at the wall. Puckett's best glove work came in Game 6 of the 1991 World Series. In the 8th inning, he saved the game and the Series for the Twins by leaping high against the outfield wall to rob an extra base hit. In the bottom of the 11th, he smashed a home run to win the game. Puckett was always smiling when he played baseball. He helped the Twins win two World Series titles, making his fans smile as well.

TWINS

KIRBY PUCKETT

▸ Outfield

HEIGHT: 5-8 **WEIGHT:** 210 lbs.
BATS: Right **THROWS:** Right
BORN: 03/14/1961 in Chicago, Ill.
SCOUTING REPORT: Perennial All-Star for his hitting as well as spectacular defense in center field.

FACT

As Minnesota Twins centerfielders, Kirby Puckett won five Gold Gloves and Torii Hunter won six.

HEIGHT: 5-11 **WEIGHT:** 150 lbs.
BATS: Both **THROWS:** Right
BORN: 12/26/1954 in Mobile, Ala.
SCOUTING REPORT: Uses his athleticism to make acrobatic plays that look impossible.

CARDINALS
OZZIE SMITH
► Shortstop

When ► **Ozzie Smith** would take the field for the first time each season he'd run out to shortstop and then spin into a cartwheel that launched him high in the air, flipping over to land squarely on his feet. That sort of athletic and acrobatic ability was also used to make unbelievable defensive plays year after year. He became known as "The Wizard of Oz" for his ability to make plays that seemed nearly magical. On April 20th, 1978, he made a diving snag with his bare hand that is still considered one of the best defensive plays of all time. He won a record 13 Gold Glove awards as a shortstop and was an All-Star 15 times.

It takes dedication to master the craft of catching Major League pitchers, and no one did it better than ► **Johnny Bench.** Bench was a prolific hitter who won the NL Rookie of the Year award in 1968 and

REDS
JOHNNY BENCH
► Catcher

HEIGHT: 6-1 **WEIGHT:** 208 lbs.
BATS: Right **THROWS:** Right
BORN: 12/07/1947 in Oklahoma City, Okla.
SCOUTING REPORT: Great athlete excels at the catching position but can also play a mean first or third base.

the NL MVP in 1970 and 1972. Behind the plate, he was the first catcher to wear a protective helmet on defense, and he popularized catching one-handed with a hinged mitt. Bench had huge hands that could each hold seven baseballs at once. While Bench's bat struck fear in opposing pitchers, base stealers dreaded his strong right arm. Bench was one of the game's best at throwing runners out. He collected a total of 10 Gold Gloves and was an All-Star 14 times.

▸ **Willie Mays** could hit for average and power, run, and throw. He is tied with Roberto Clemente for the most Gold Gloves as an outfielder with 12. Mays had speed that allowed him to cover enormous territory in the outfield. On September 29, 1954—Game 1 of the World Series—he made a play that is known today as simply "The Catch." In a tie game, Vic Wertz of the Cleveland Indians launched a fly ball to deep center field. Mays turned and ran with amazing speed to catch up to the ball and reached out his glove to make an over-the-shoulder catch. It was one of the best plays ever, by one of the best outfielders ever to play the game.

GIANTS

WILLIE MAYS
▸Outfield

HEIGHT: 5-10 **WEIGHT:** 170 lbs.
BATS: Right **THROWS:** Right
BORN: 05/06/1931 in Westfield, Ala.
SCOUTING REPORT: As graceful as a dancer in center field and covers a tremendous amount of territory.

CHAPTER SIX

SIX DEGREES OF AROLDIS CHAPMAN

MARIANO RIVERA
Reached 200 saves faster than anyone, until Papelbon broke that record.

JONATHAN PAPELBON
Recorded final ninth-inning out of the 2012 All-Star Game for the NL after Chapman closed eighth inning.

TREVOR HOFFMAN
Career saves leader until Rivera surpassed him.

ROLLIE FINGERS
Padres career saves leader until Hoffman passed him.

DENNIS ECKERSLEY
Broke Fingers' team career saves record as an Oakland Athletic.

RELIABLE RELIEVERS

With the game on the line, you want someone to dominate the opposing team, if only for a few outs. The men who make their living in the eighth and ninth innings have to have nerves of steel and supreme confidence in their ability to get batters out. These are baseball's best closers.

AROLDIS CHAPMAN
▶ Relievers

HEIGHT: 6-4 **WEIGHT:** 205 lbs.
BATS: Right **THROWS:** Left
BORN: 02/28/1988 in Holguin, Cuba
SCOUTING REPORT: The "Cuban Missile" throws a flaming fastball and racks up strikeouts and saves with ease.

At just 21 years old, ▶ **Aroldis Chapman** walked away from the Cuban national team during the World Baseball Classic, leaving his homeland for a chance at the Major Leagues. He wouldn't be disappointed. The Cincinnati Reds took a chance on the tall, lanky lefty and watched him blossom into the hardest throwing pitcher in MLB history.

He holds the record for the fastest pitch ever recorded in a MLB game with a 105.1-mile-per-hour heater against the San Diego Padres on September 25, 2010. Against the Arizona Diamondbacks in 2014 he unleashed 15 fastballs that were each clocked over 100 mph. While he does have a nasty slider, the three-time All-Star relies on his blazing fastball to strike out hitters and notch save after save for the Reds.

▶ **Jonathan Papelbon** wanted to be a starter. But when pressed into duty as the Red Sox closer, he found that the end of games, not the beginning, were his best fit. A fiery competitor, his fastball seems to jump out of his hand. When hitters look for it, Papelbon sneaks in a splitter that dives at the plate to fool them. He saved three games in the 2007 World Series for the Red Sox. In 2011 he

PHILLIES

JONATHAN PAPELBON

▶ Reliever

HEIGHT: 6-4 **WEIGHT:** 215 lbs.
BATS: Right **THROWS:** Right
BORN: 11/23/1980 in Baton Rouge, La.
SCOUTING REPORT: Electric fastball and a diving splitter renders hitters helpless.

reached his 200th save in just his 359th appearance, surpassing the record set by legendary closer Mariano Rivera of the Yankees.

When ▶ **Mariano Rivera** took the mound in the ninth inning for the New York Yankees, opponents knew they were in trouble. A fierce competitor, Rivera always seemed cool and in control on the mound. Rivera's signature pitch was the cut fastball, a pitch that looked like a normal fastball but dashed right to left as it crossed the plate. The result was that batters struggled to make solid contact and many, many bats would break. He appeared in seven World Series, recording 11 saves with an ERA of 0.99. He retired after the 2013 season as the all-time saves leader with 652 saves.

YANKEES

MARIANO RIVERA

▶ Reliever

HEIGHT: 6-2 **WEIGHT:** 195 lbs.
BATS: Right **THROWS:** Right
BORN: 11/29/1969 in Panama City, Panama
SCOUTING REPORT: The all-time saves leader demolishes bats with his cutter.

PADRES

TREVOR HOFFMAN

▶ Reliever

HEIGHT: 6-1 **WEIGHT:** 200 lbs.
BATS: Right **THROWS:** Right
BORN: 10/13/1967 in Bellflower, Calif.
SCOUTING REPORT: Master at keeping hitters off balance and keeping leads safe features an exemplary changeup.

▶ **Trevor Hoffman** was drafted as a shortstop with a cannon of an arm. His hitting never lived up to the potential of his arm, so his coaches turned him into a relief pitcher. Hoffman blossomed on the mound. His fastball rarely hit 90 miles per hour, but his change-up was deadly. His changeup looked just like a fastball but travelled at 73 to 76 miles per hour and then dipped sharply as it reached the plate. He was the first closer to reach 500 saves, and then he eclipsed 600 saves as well.

▶ **Rollie Fingers** was known as much for his trademark handlebar mustache as he was for shutting teams down in the late innings. Early in his career Fingers struggled as a starter. His manager, Dick Williams, moved him to the bullpen and eventually realized that he was particularly effective at the end of games while protecting a lead. Fingers is still

ATHLETICS

ROLLIE FINGERS

▶ Reliever

HEIGHT: 6-4 **WEIGHT:** 190 lbs.
BATS: Right **THROWS:** Right
BORN: 08/25/1946 in Steubenville, Ohio
SCOUTING REPORT: Wearer of the most recognizable mustache in baseball is one of the first to embrace a late-innings role with great success.

considered one of baseball's first true closers. His sharp slider was an effective strikeout pitch. In 1981 he was so effective as a closer that he won the AL Cy Young Award and the AL MVP. His number 34 was retired by both the Milwaukee Brewers and the Oakland Athletics.

▸ **Dennis Eckersley** looked like a wild man with a mustache and long hair spilling out of his cap. After several years as a moderately successful starter, Eckersley moved to the bullpen and became one of the most feared closers in baseball. He is the only player to pitch 100 complete games and have more than 100 saves. Eckersley pounded the strike zone, walking only 86 batters during the last 10 years of his career. He dared hitters to hit his live fastball and sweeping slider. More often than not, they couldn't. Eckersley embraced the role of closer, saying, "When I started finishing games and coming off the field shaking hands, it was a beautiful thing."

ATHLETICS

DENNIS ECKERSLEY

▸Reliever and Starting Pitcher

HEIGHT: 6-2 **WEIGHT:** 190 lbs.
BATS: Right **THROWS:** Right
BORN: 10/03/54 in Oakland, Calif.
SCOUTING REPORT: Though he looks like a wild man, Eck pounds the strike zone with a good fastball and nasty slider.

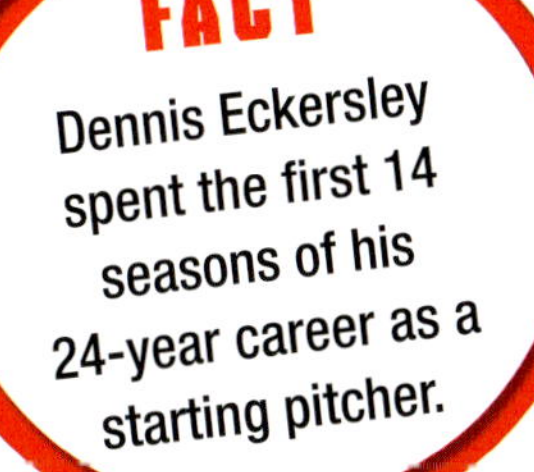

FACT

Dennis Eckersley spent the first 14 seasons of his 24-year career as a starting pitcher.

SIX DEGREES TRIVIA

MATCH THE PLAYER WITH HIS NICKNAME:

1.	WILLIE MAYS	THE IRON HORSE
2.	OZZIE SMITH	CUBAN MISSILE
3.	SANDY KOUFAX	THE MACHINE
4.	CLAYTON KERSHAW	LITTLE GENERAL
5.	DAVID ORTIZ	SAY HEY KID
6.	DEREK JETER	THE FRANCHISE
7.	BABE RUTH	BIG PAPI
8.	ALBERT PUJOLS	THE SULTAN OF SWAT
9.	TY COBB	VINCENT VAN GO
10.	VINCE COLEMAN	HAMMERIN' HANK
11.	MARIANO RIVERA	MR. OCTOBER
12.	AROLDIS CHAPMAN	THE LEFT ARM OF GOD
13.	TORII HUNTER	MUDDY CHICKEN
14.	JOHNNY BENCH	CAPTAIN CLUTCH
15.	DUSTIN PEDROIA	THE JUDGE
16.	CY YOUNG	THE SANDMAN
17.	HENRY AARON	SPIDER-MAN
18.	REGGIE JACKSON	CYCLONE
19.	FRANK ROBINSON	THE CLAW
20.	LOU BROCK	THE GEORGIA PEACH
21.	LOU GEHRIG	THE WIZARD

Answers:

1. Say Hey Kid, 2. The Wizard, 3. The Left Arm of God, 4. The Claw, 5. Big Papi, 6. Captain Clutch, 7. The Sultan of Swat, 8. The Machine, 9. The Georgia Peach, 10. Vincent Van Go, 11. The Sandman, 12. Cuban Missile, 13. Spider-Man, 14. Little General, 15. Muddy Chicken, 16. Cyclone, 17 Hammerin' Hank, 18. Mr. October, 19. The Judge, 20. The Franchise, 21. The Iron Horse

USING THE WORD BANK OF NAMES, ANSWER EACH QUESTION

David Ortiz · Cy Young · Mariano Rivera · Mike Trout · Dustin Pedroia · Clayton Kershaw · Torii Hunter · Cal Ripken Jr. · Justin Verlander · Ty Cobb · Derek Jeter · Nolan Ryan · Rollie Fingers · Satchel Paige · Jacoby Ellsbury · Rickey Henderson · Kirby Puckett · Jonathan Papelbon · Frank Robinson · Ozzie Smith · Vince Coleman · Reggie Jackson · Hank Aaron · Sandy Koufax · Johnny Bench · Jim Thome · Aroldis Chapman · Willie Mays · Lou Gehrig · Albert Pujols · Miguel Cabrera · Babe Ruth · Lou Brock · Trevor Hoffman · Dennis Eckersley

1. Which seven players in this book are members of the 3,000 hit club?
2. Which five pitchers have won an MVP award?
3. Which six retired players played their whole careers with just one team?
4. Which five players made their Major League debut while still in their teens?
5. Which four pitchers have had fastballs clocked at 100 mph or faster?
6. Which eight players were first-round picks in the Amateur Baseball Draft?
7. Which player has played in both the college and MLB World Series?
8. Which five players were born outside the United States?

Answers:

1. Ty Cobb, Hank Aaron, Derek Jeter, Willie Mays, Cal Ripken Jr., Rickey Henderson, Lou Brock
2. Sandy Koufax, Rollie Fingers, Dennis Eckersley, Justin Verlander, Clayton Kershaw
3. Sandy Koufax, Kirby Puckett, Cal Ripken Jr., Lou Gehrig, Johnny Bench, Mariano Rivera
4. Babe Ruth, Ty Cobb, Mike Trout, Nolan Ryan, Sandy Koufax
5. Justin Verlander, Nolan Ryan, Jonathan Papelbon, Aroldis Chapman
6. Andrew McCutchen, Mike Trout, Derek Jeter, Jacoby Ellsbury, Justin Verlander,Torii Hunter, Kirby Puckett, Clayton Kershaw
7. Jacoby Ellsbury
8. Miguel Cabrera, David Ortiz, Albert Pujols, Mariano Rivera, Aroldis Chapman

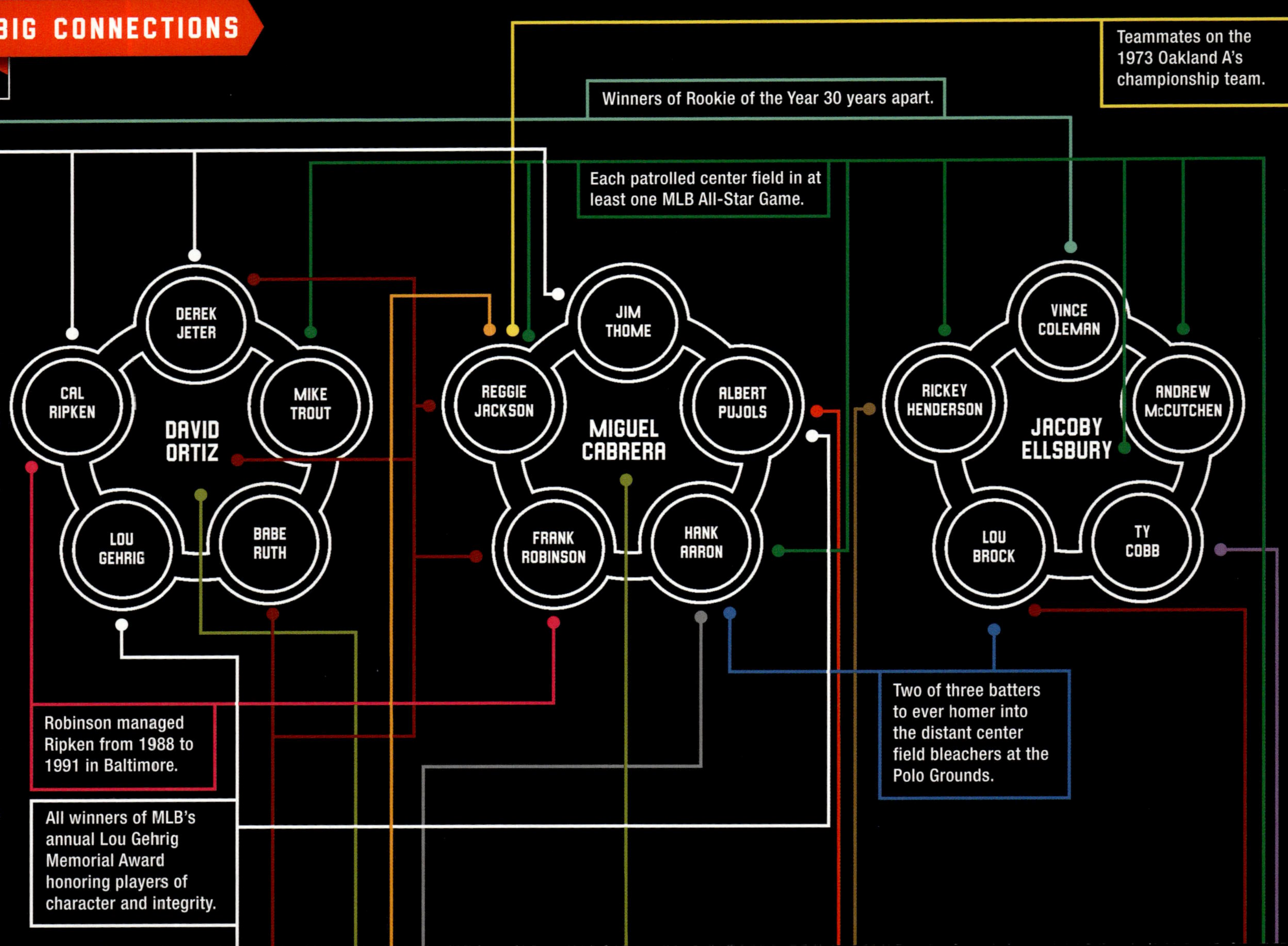
Teammates on the 1973 Oakland A's championship team.
Winners of Rookie of the Year 30 years apart.
Each patrolled center field in at least one MLB All-Star Game.
DEREK JETER
CAL RIPKEN
MIKE TROUT
DAVID ORTIZ
LOU GEHRIG
BABE RUTH
JIM THOME
REGGIE JACKSON
ALBERT PUJOLS
MIGUEL CABRERA
FRANK ROBINSON
HANK AARON
VINCE COLEMAN
RICKEY HENDERSON
ANDREW McCUTCHEN
JACOBY ELLSBURY
LOU BROCK
TY COBB
Robinson managed Ripken from 1988 to 1991 in Baltimore.
All winners of MLB's annual Lou Gehrig Memorial Award honoring players of character and integrity.
Two of three batters to ever homer into the distant center field bleachers at the Polo Grounds.

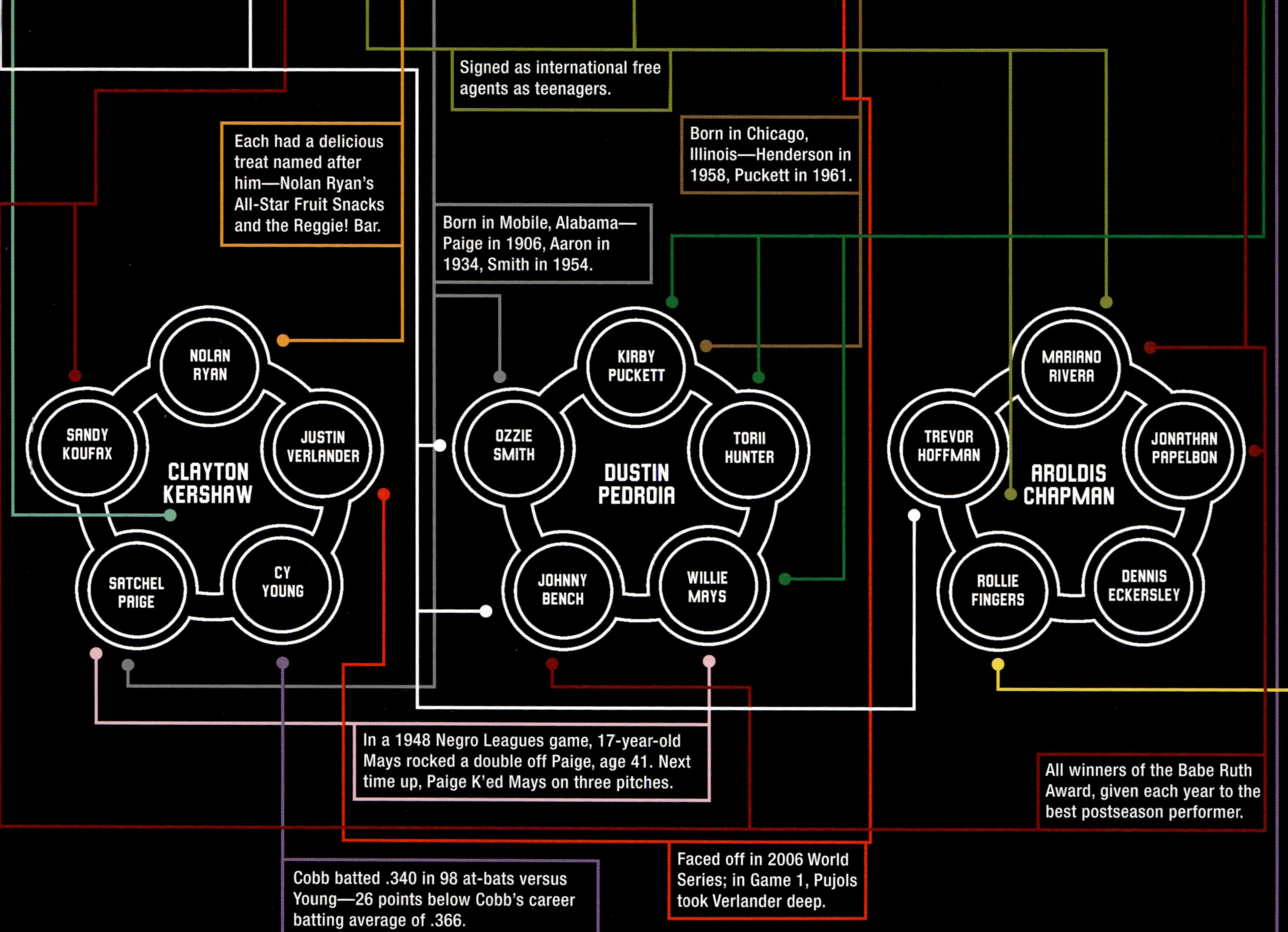

Signed as international free agents as teenagers.
Each had a delicious treat named after him—Nolan Ryan's All-Star Fruit Snacks and the Reggie! Bar.
Born in Chicago, Illinois—Henderson in 1958, Puckett in 1961.
Born in Mobile, Alabama—Paige in 1906, Aaron in 1934, Smith in 1954.
NOLAN RYAN
SANDY KOUFAX
JUSTIN VERLANDER
CLAYTON KERSHAW
SATCHEL PAIGE
CY YOUNG
KIRBY PUCKETT
OZZIE SMITH
TORII HUNTER
DUSTIN PEDROIA
JOHNNY BENCH
WILLIE MAYS
MARIANO RIVERA
TREVOR HOFFMAN
JONATHAN PAPELBON
AROLDIS CHAPMAN
ROLLIE FINGERS
DENNIS ECKERSLEY
In a 1948 Negro Leagues game, 17-year-old Mays rocked a double off Paige, age 41. Next time up, Paige K'ed Mays on three pitches.
All winners of the Babe Ruth Award, given each year to the best postseason performer.
Cobb batted .340 in 98 at-bats versus Young—26 points below Cobb's career batting average of .366.
Faced off in 2006 World Series; in Game 1, Pujols took Verlander deep.

GLOSSARY

ace—a team's best pitcher; usually the first pitcher to take a turn in the starting rotation

cutter—a kind of fastball that breaks slightly left or right before reaching home plate

designated hitter—a player who takes a turn in the batting order but does not play the field

Gold Glove—annual award given to the best fielders at each fielding position in both the National League and the American League

RBI—stands for run batted in

reliever—a pitcher who is used to take over for the pitcher who starts the game

save—a relief pitcher may earn a save by keeping a team's lead when replacing another pitcher at the end of a game

splitter—a split-finger fastball, thrown with the fingers spread wide which makes the ball drop suddenly as it approaches home plate

strike zone—the area over home plate the ball must pass through to be called a strike

READ MORE

Bryant, Howard. *Legends: The Best Players, Games, and Teams in Baseball.* New York: Philomel Books, 2015.

Chandler, Matt. *Side-by-Side Baseball Stars: Comparing Pro Baseball's Greatest Players* (Side-by-Side Sports). North Mankato, Minn.: Capstone Press, 2014.

LeBoutillier, Nate. *The Ultimate Guide to Pro Baseball Teams.* North Mankato, Minn.: Capstone Press, 2011.

INTERNET SITES

FactHound offers a safe, fun way to find Internet sites related to this book. All of the sites on FactHound have been researched by our staff.

Here's all you do:

Visit *www.facthound.com*

Type in this code: 9781491421420

Check out projects, games and lots more at
www.capstonekids.com

INDEX